Night Night Hamlet

Written by CLINT PLYLER

Illustrated by TAMI BOYCE

ISBN-13: 978-0-692-18569-8
Clint Plyler Publishing
Dover, PA

To the people of Carbondale, Pennsylvania,
along with my wife and children,
the God of the hills and valleys has
blessed you with great beauty.

"My beautiful cubs want to go to town but I am warm and have settled in.

How can I say no to beautiful eyes and big grins?"

"Grab your things my sweets, we will walk and get some treats," said Papa.

"Yay!" said Penny and Maya.

"Put on your hat, coat, and boots," Momma said with a smile.

"You can see the town from up here.
The stores, the streets, the places to eat,
all down below," said Maya.

"Come on Papa, keep up,
you're getting slow," joked Penny.

"Look in this window,
what is your wish?" asked Papa.

"That ring for Momma,
That ball bat for me," said Penny.

HONEYSUCKLE DINER

That tool for you Papa,
and that hat for me," said Maya.

"Are you hungry?
Honey Suckle Diner has the best sweets!"

"Pull up a chair and take off your stuff.

How about some cake or a cream puff?" asked Polar Bear waiter.

"Hot chocolate for the cubs and hot tea for me," said Papa Bear.

For a little extra money, I can stir in some honey" said the Polar Bear.

"Cake would be nice," said Penny. "Do that twice!" said Maya.

Big eyes and wide grins met cakes that were not thin from the Polar Bear waiter.

"Girls, you ate your cake and I drank my tea with extra honey.

Time to leave, but first let us leave some money."

Leaving the diner, the cubs saw different houses.

A den for a fox.
A hole for a mouse.
A tree for a squirrel,
And a grand ole house.

Penny's eyes opened wide as she said "Momma would love to live in this house!"

"Please, can we go to the great tree?"
asked Maya.

Papa replied with a grin, "Okay."

Seeing the church steeple, Maya asked,
"Does anyone live high on the top?"

"No dear, only birds visit that spot,"
said Papa.

"Brrr! It's cold," Papa said.
"Let's leave the hamlet and go to bed."

Momma said, "Into the den and off with your stuff,
time for good night prayers, and pillows with fluff."

Momma and Papa tucked them in tight.

Warm in their beds, they whispered, "Good night."

"But what is a hamlet?" asked Maya from her bed.

"It's a little town," replied Momma "now lay down your head."

"Night, night little hamlet," whispered Maya and Penny.

"Night, night little girls," replied Momma and Papa.

MEET the AUTHOR and ILLUSTRATOR

 **CLINT PLYLER** is a Southern born writer with a northern home. Born and raised in South Carolina, he now lives in Pennsylvania with his wife April and three children. You will often find him at the nearest coffee shop writing or sketching. Educated in both design and pastoral ministries, he is equally passionate about designing products, writing books, and engaging in a good discussion about theology. When he is not working, you will find him exploring the great outdoors. Yes, he eats southern style grits and loves good pizza from a Pennsylvania pizzeria.

 **TAMI BOYCE** is a Charleston-based illustrator and graphic designer with a fun and whimsical style. She has possessed a love of drawing for as long as she can remember, and Tami considers herself lucky to be able to incorporate what she loves into her career. To see more of Tami's work, please visit tamiboyce.com.